SPOTLIGHT ON GEORGIA

# GEORGIA FROM WORLD WAR I THROUGH THE GREAT DEPRESSION

SAM CROMPTON

NEW YORK

Published in 2018 by The Rosen Publishing Group, Inc.
29 East 21st Street, New York, NY 10010



Editor: Theresa Morlock
Book Design: Michael Flynn
Interior Layout: Rachel Rising

Photo Credits: Cover, p. 29 Bettmann/Bettmann/Getty Images; p. 5 Reinhold Leitner/Shutterstock.com; pp. 5, 13, 23 Everett Historical/Shutterstock.com; p. 6 https://commons.wikimedia.org/wiki/File:HMS_Otranto_IWM_SP_001064.jpg#/media/File:HMS_Otranto_IWM_SP_001064.jpg; p. 7 https://en.wikipedia.org/wiki/File:Emergency_hospital_during_Influenza_epidemic,_Camp_Funston,_Kansas_-_NCP_1603.jpg#/media/File:Emergency_hospital_during_Influenza_epidemic,_Camp_Funston,_Kansas_-_NCP_1603.jpg; p. 9 Courtesy of Berrien County, Georgia Photos; p. 11 Jansen Chua/Shutterstock.com; p. 15 https://an.wikipedia.org/wiki/Gran_Depresi%C3%B3n#/media/File:Poor_mother_and_children,_Oklahoma,_1936_by_Dorothea_Lange.jpg; p. 17 Charles Phelps Cushing/ClassicStock/Archive Photos/Getty Images; p. 18 Photo Researchers/Science Source/Getty Images; p. 19 https://en.wikipedia.org/wiki/Little_White_House#/media/File:USA-Georgia-Warm_Springs-Roosevelt%27s_Little_White_House.JPG; p. 21 https://commons.wikimedia.org/wiki/File:Fort_Hawkins_Macon,_Georgia.jpg; p. 21 (inset) https://commons.wikimedia.org/wiki/File:15_28_001_hawkins.jpg; p. 22 Interim Archive/ Archive Photos/Getty Images; p. 25 Jason Patrick Ross/Shutterstock.com; p. 27 https://commons.wikimedia.org/wiki/File:Signing_Of_The_Social_Security_Act.jpg.

Cataloging-in-Publication Data
Names: Crompton, Sam.
Title: Georgia from World War I through the Great Depression / Sam Crompton.
Description: New York : PowerKids Press, 2018. | Series: Spotlight on Georgia | Includes index.
Identifiers: ISBN 9781508159865 (pbk.) | ISBN 9781508159896 (library bound) | ISBN 9781508159872 (6 pack)
Subjects: LCSH: Georgia--History--Juvenile literature.
Classification: LCC F286.3 C76 2018 | DDC 975.8--dc23

Manufactured in the United States of America

CPSIA Compliance Information: Batch #BS17PK For further information contact Rosen Publishing, New York, New York at 1-800-237-9932.

# CONTENTS

# CHAPTER ONE

# GEORGIA DURING WWI

World War I began in 1914 as a conflict between the Allies, made up mainly of Great Britain, France, Russia, Italy, and Japan, and the Central Powers, made up mainly of Germany, Austria-Hungary, and Turkey. By 1917, the United States joined the fight alongside the Allies.

Georgians were quick to lend their support to the war effort. Thousands of men and women served in the military. Georgia had more military training camps than any other state. Georgia mills made fabric for military uniforms, and railroads transported weapons and supplies. Georgia farms also grew food and cotton for the U.S military.

Although many people volunteered to serve, America needed more troops. The Selective Service Act, which took effect in May 1917, required all American men ages 21 to 30 to register for the **draft**. More than 500,000 men from Georgia registered.

Men Wanted for the Army

APPLY AT

In Georgia, many white landowners depended on the work of African American laborers. To keep African Americans from leaving Georgia to serve in the war, they hid draft notices from them or tried to stop them from registering.

# CHAPTER TWO

# WARTIME LOSSES

Georgia suffered many losses throughout the war, some of which were unrelated to battle. One of the most unexpected losses occurred when the HMS *Otranto* crashed into another ship during a storm in the Irish Sea. When the *Otranto* sank, 130 soldiers from Georgia who were onboard lost their lives.

*The Otranto* accident claimed the lives of over 370 men.

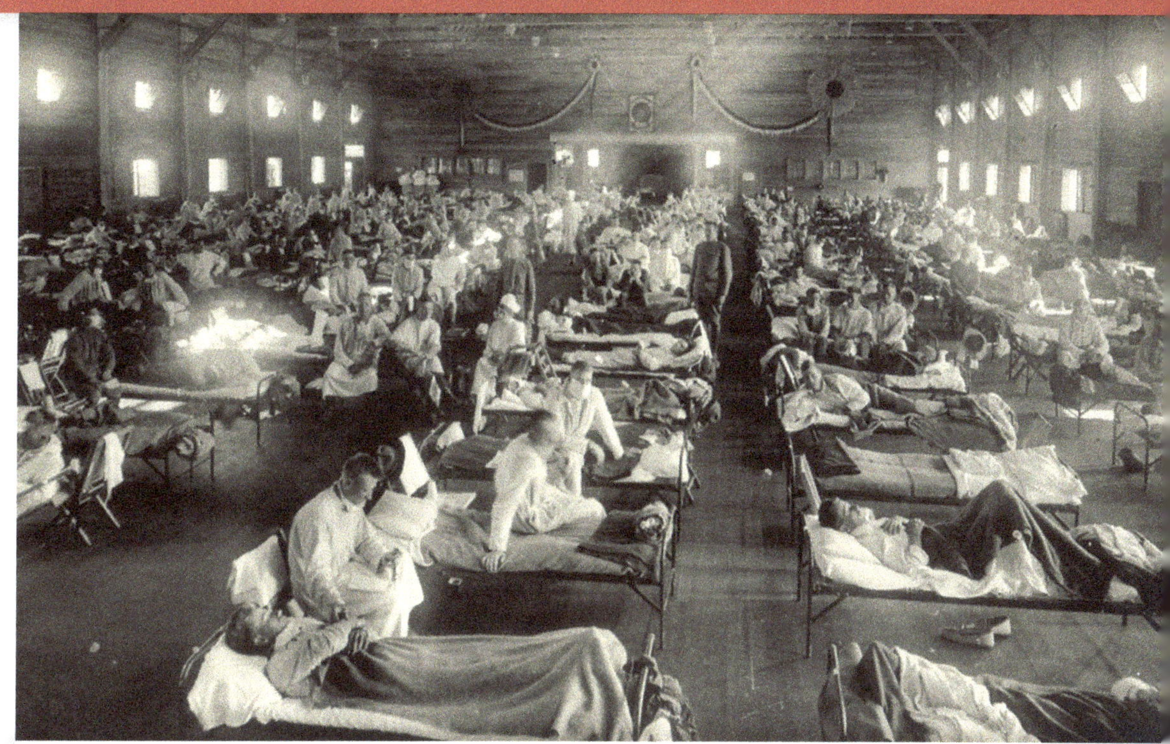

During the influenza pandemic, emergency hospitals were set up to treat the sick.

Many people were also lost to the influenza **pandemic**, which hit in 1918. This type of influenza, which was also called the Spanish flu, was very **contagious**. It spread very quickly within Georgia's military training camps. Within the course of a single day, more than 50 Georgian soldiers lost their lives to it. Across the country, other states suffered even greater losses. Over 600,000 Americans would die of influenza before the pandemic was over. The influenza pandemic was responsible for more deaths than World War I.

# CHAPTER THREE

# WAR'S END

When the United States entered the war in 1917, the odds tipped in favor of the Allied forces. With help from the Americans, the Allies were able to defeat the Central Powers. World War I officially ended on November 11, 1918. The war brought about lasting changes, and its influence would continue to be felt for decades to come.

World War I and its aftermath had an enormous effect on life in America. Georgia became home to many military training camps and contributed thousands of soldiers to the war effort. Georgia's industries supplied the troops with food and uniforms and transported weapons. Georgia's population changed as a result of the draft and job opportunities in northern cities, which drew many African American Georgians. Georgia's economy would continue to feel the effects of World War I for decades after the war's end.

A sculpture called *The Spirit of the American Doughboy* was placed in Nashville, Georgia, and other cities across the country to honor the memory of American soldiers lost in WWI.

CHAPTER FOUR

# THE BOLL WEEVIL OUTBREAK

During the early 1900s, Georgia's economy depended heavily on the production of cotton. Large cotton plantations covered 5.2 million acres (2.1 ha) of Georgia land. Beginning in 1914, an outbreak of boll weevils wrecked the cotton crop, destroying Georgia's economy.

Boll weevils are small beetles that eat cotton buds and flowers. During this time, the weevils **migrated** north from Central America, eating cotton plants at enormous rates. Whole fields of cotton simply disappeared. Greene County, Georgia, suffered the worst, but across the state cotton production dropped by 66 percent. By 1923, the cotton acreage had dropped to 2.6 million acres (1.05 million ha).

The boll weevil outbreak permanently damaged Georgia's cotton industry. Farmers realized that it was important to diversify, or plant different crops, instead of totally depending on cotton. Farmers used **pesticides** to help control the problem, but the fight against boll weevils would continue for many years.

The National Boll Weevil Eradication Program was created during the 1970s and has successfully removed boll weevils from many areas.

# CHAPTER FIVE

# DROUGHT AND MIGRATION

During the war, many African American Georgians moved north to find jobs. The boll weevil outbreak made farm work scarce and many people were able to find factory jobs in the north producing supplies for the war. In 1924, a **drought** struck Georgia, which pushed even more African Americans to northern cities. In Georgia, many African Americans worked as **sharecroppers**. The drought hit farmers the hardest, drying up their fields and killing their crops. During the drought, many sharecroppers and poor farmers were forced to sell their land and look for work in northern cities. Moving north also appealed to African Americans wishing to escape the **discrimination** they experienced in the south.

This mass movement of southern African Americans to northern cities from 1916 to 1970 is called the Great Migration. More than 6 million African Americans moved north during the Great Migration. Many settled in Chicago, Detroit, and New York.

Under the sharecropping system, workers had no opportunity to improve their lifestyles or earn more money for their families. In northern cities, they could find factory jobs where they could earn a livable wage.

# CHAPTER SIX

# THE STOCK MARKET CRASH

The combined effects of the boll weevil outbreak and the drought led to an economic depression in Georgia. This economic depression was a time of poor economy, a drop in spending, and widespread unemployment. With the **stock market** crash of October 1929, the rest of the country followed Georgia into the Great Depression.

Throughout most of the 1920s, the stock market grew stronger. It began to drop in September 1929. By October many investors had taken their money back, causing the market to crash. Millions of Americans had money in the stock market and when share prices fell, companies went out of business. Common people suffered because they lost jobs. In addition, the value of money decreased, meaning people couldn't afford to buy the things they needed and there was little demand for the products many companies sold.

By 1930, more than 3.2 million people in the United States were unemployed.

# CHAPTER SEVEN

# THE HOOVER YEARS

Herbert Hoover took office as the president of the United States in 1929. Before he entered politics, Hoover had made a lot of money as a mining engineer. His efforts to help send food and supplies to Europe during World War I earned him admiration from American citizens. Hoover had also served the country well while working under previous presidents.

When the stock market crashed, Hoover's attitude was that Americans needed to solve the situation without the help of the federal government. He approved some policies to help the economy but feared that expanding the federal government would be harmful to the country in the long run.

Many Americans saw President Hoover as cruel, believing that his lack of action meant that he ignored their suffering. During his term, without aid from the federal government, conditions in America grew much worse. In 1932, Franklin D. Roosevelt was elected president to replace Hoover.

Many people lost their homes during the Great Depression and built shacks to live in. These shack towns came to be called "Hoovervilles" after the president.

# CHAPTER EIGHT

# FDR IN GEORGIA

President Roosevelt, commonly called FDR, was very popular in Georgia. Before he became president, FDR had a disease called polio. The effects of this disease prevented him from walking. He came to a health resort in Warm Springs to recover. The water at Warm Springs was believed to have healing abilities and FDR swam there to exercise his legs.

FRANKLIN DELANO ROOSEVELT

LITTLE WHITE HOUSE IN WARM SPRINGS

FDR was at the Little White House when he passed away on April 12, 1945.

Roosevelt visited Warm Springs so frequently that he had a home built there. During his presidency, he came to this home as a retreat from his demanding political life. Georgians formed a bond with the president because he was often seen in public, driving his car through the countryside and waving to people passing by. Although FDR was from New York, he shared a special connection with the people of Georgia.

# CHAPTER NINE

# THE NEW DEAL

Unlike President Hoover, FDR put plans into place to use the federal government to solve the issues of the Great Depression. FDR's program was called the New Deal. Between 1933 and 1939, under the New Deal, plans were **enacted** to offer economic relief and improve agriculture, labor, and housing.

During the first 100 days of his presidency, FDR created a series of reforms and bills with the aim of ending the Great Depression. The Works Progress Administration (WPA) was a relief program designed to give jobless Americans work again. The WPA employed over 8.5 million people, who built public buildings, bridges, roads, and parks that are still in use today. Of the many New Deal plans, the Civilian Conservation Corps, the Agricultural Adjustment Act, the Social Security Act, and the Rural Electrification Act had some of the greatest impacts on Georgia.

A replica of Fort Hawkins in Macon County, Georgia, was built by the WPA and completed in 1938. The original Fort Hawkins was a military post built in 1806.

# CHAPTER TEN

# THE AGRICULTURAL ADJUSTMENT ACT

In 1933, Congress passed the Agricultural Adjustment Act (AAA). The goal of the AAA was to repair the damage to American agriculture caused by the Great Depression. To do so, the AAA cut farm production and raised the price of goods. By limiting agricultural production, the government hoped to increase demand for products. As demand increased, prices rose, giving farmers a livable income. The AAA also established banks and provided loans to farmers. By the late 1930s, many were able to afford advanced farm tools such as tractors.

The AAA was also called the Farm Relief Bill. Farmers met with government workers to determine how the bill would apply to their land.

Unfortunately, sharecroppers didn't experience the benefits of the AAA. Production cuts meant there was less land available to farm, and new farming tools could do some of the work that had once been done by sharecroppers. In 1936, the Supreme Court declared the AAA unconstitutional. An improved Agricultural Adjustment Act was passed in 1938.

# CHAPTER ELEVEN

# THE CIVILIAN CONSERVATION CORPS

The Civilian Conservation Corps (CCC) was established in 1933. The CCC was designed to employ young men in their 20s and 30s. The men would work under the Departments of Labor, War, and Agriculture on projects to plant trees, create parks, and keep forest trails in order. Workers lived in on-site camps and sent their earnings home to their families. The CCC employed over 3 million men and was very effective in Georgia.

More than 78,000 Georgian men worked for the CCC between 1933 and 1942. They built dams, planted millions of trees, and set up telephone lines. Several state parks were created in Georgia, as well as many new roads and bridges.

Work camps were separated by race. Discrimination in Georgia might've prevented African Americans from sharing the benefits of the CCC if the Labor Department had not insisted on their involvement.

One of the CCC's many lasting **legacies** is the Appalachian Trail. Georgian CCC workers built the stone shelter at the top of the Blood Mountain part of the trail.

# CHAPTER TWELVE

# THE SOCIAL SECURITY ACT

In 1935, Congress passed the Social Security Act. Under this act, taxes are collected from working people and their employers to provide security for unemployed and elderly people and others in need. Before the Social Security Act, elderly people depended on their families to support them after retirement, which meant that many faced poverty and homelessness. Under the Social Security Act, retired adults receive payments to help them support themselves. Unemployed people and dependent children are also provided for under the terms of the act.

The Social Security Act changed the government's relationship with American citizens. Many disapproved of these changes, feeling that the government shouldn't interfere with people's lives. Some felt that to be strong, American citizens must be expected to provide for themselves without assistance.

FDR signed the Social Security Act on August 14, 1935.

# CHAPTER THIRTEEN

# EUGENE TALMADGE

Eugene Talmadge, a popular Georgia politician, opposed the New Deal. Born in Forsyth in 1884, Talmadge rose slowly in the Democratic Party ranks. He became secretary of commerce in 1926 and was famous for his temper and style. Talmadge claimed he was there to help the common person, by which he meant the white, working Georgians who lived in the countryside.

Talmadge served two terms as governor. He used racial **prejudice** to create public outcry against New Deal reforms. He prevented African Americans from enlisting in New Deal programs, and he spoke out against FDR. Although Talmadge wasn't able to stop New Deal programs in Georgia, his resistance did slow their progress. He tried to stop FDR from being reelected as president but failed. FDR began his second term in 1936. He was reelected in 1940 and 1944, serving 12 years as president.

Talmadge was a white supremacist, meaning he thought that white people were better than people of other races.

# CHAPTER FOURTEEN

# YEARS OF STRUGGLE

Life in Georgia from World War I through the Great Depression was a struggle for most. The boll weevil outbreak, drought, influenza pandemic, and World War I took their toll on the population and economy of the state. Long before the Great Depression hit the country in 1929, Georgia had been suffering economically.

The Great Depression ended in 1939. During that year, a second world war erupted in Europe. In America, more jobs were created to prepare to defend the country from attack and to send aid to Britain and France. When the United States joined the war in 1941, life for Georgians changed again. Demand for products and labor rose. Another draft was imposed and many people joined the military. World War II opened new possibilities to women and African Americans in Georgia and lead to industrial **modernization**, which improved conditions in the state in the years ahead.

# GLOSSARY

**contagious (kuhn-TAY-juhs)** Able to be passed on.

**discrimination (duh-skrih-muh-NAY-shun)** Different—usually unfair—treatment based on factors such as a person's race, age, religion, or gender.

**draft (DRAFT)** The system of selecting people for required military service.

**drought (DROWT)** A period of dryness during which there is very little or no rain.

**enact (uh-NAKT)** To put into place or bring about.

**legacy (LEH-guh-see)** The lasting effect of a person or thing.

**migrate (MY-grayt)** To move from one place to another.

**modernization (mah-duhr-nuh-ZAY-shun)** The process of changing to fit modern demands.

**pandemic (pan-DEH-mik)** A sickness that quickly spreads over a whole country or the world.

**pesticide (PES-tuh-syd)** A poison used to kill pests.

**prejudice (PREH-juh-dis)** An unfair feeling of dislike for a person or group because of race or religious or political beliefs.

**sharecropper (SHEHR-krah-puhr)** People who farm land they do not own and share the crops with the landowner.

**stock market (STAHK MAR-ket)** A market for buying shares, or part ownership, in companies.

# INDEX



# PRIMARY SOURCE LIST

**Page 13**
Thirteen-year-old African American sharecropper boy plowing. Photograph. Created by Dorothea Lange. July 1937.

**Page 23**
A Nebraska farmer meets with a Farm Security Administration Debt Adjustment Committee. Photograph. Created by Arthur Rothstein. May 1936.

**Page 27**
Franklin D. Roosevelt signs the Social Security Act. Photograph. August 14, 1935. Now kept at the Library of Congress.

# WEBSITES

Due to the changing nature of Internet links, PowerKids Press has developed an online list of websites related to the subject of this book. This site is updated regularly. Please use this link to access the list: www.powerkidslinks.com/sog/dep